BIBLE DETECTIVES
Mark
Puzzle Book

Written by Ros Woodman
Illustrated by Ron Wheeler

Wordsearch Puzzles designed by Chris Woodman
Cover Design by Catherine Mackenzie
Printed and bound by Bell and Bain, Glasgow

Published by Christian Focus Publications
Geanies House, Fearn, Tain, Ross-shire, IV20 1TW, Scotland, UK.
www.christianfocus.com email: info@christianfocus.com

Intro

Hello. We're Harry and Jess. We're *The Bible Detectives Squad* and we're on a special case right now. How about joining our team? We're on an investigation through **Mark's gospel** and we've got Click our computer mouse to help. Before we start - Click has downloaded data to get us started. Show us what you found Click!

Mark
Occupation: Writer.

Mark lived in Bible times and is a bit of a mystery. It is believed that he was a close friend of Peter, the disciple, and that possibly Mark's mother is the woman mentioned in Acts Chapter 12 verse 12 who had a house in Jerusalem where the believers met together.

Gospel
Gospel is another word for Good News. Some books of the New Testament are called Gospels - Matthew, Mark, Luke and John. It also describes the good news that we read in the Bible, which is - Jesus died to save us from our sins.

The Bible

This is God's book. He used people to do the physical writing. Prophets, men of God, the disciples - all wrote down or told other people what it was that God said to them. There are two sections. **The Old Testament** happened before Jesus was born and **The New Testament** is about Jesus life, death, resurrection and what his followers did after he went back to heaven.

More Data The Old and New Testaments are divided into different sections. The Old Testament is made up of 39 separate books. The New Testament is made up of 27 different books. There are 66 books in the Bible. Each Bible book is divided up into smaller sections called chapters. Each chapter is divided up into smaller parts called verses.

Old Testament

New Testament

Old Testament: Genesis, Exodus, Leviticus, Numbers, Deuteronomy, Joshua, Judges, Ruth, 1&2 Samuel, 1&2 Kings, 1&2 Chronicles, Ezra, Nehemiah, Esther, Job, Psalms, Proverbs, Ecclesiastes, Song of Songs, Isaiah, Jeremiah, Lamentations, Ezekiel, Daniel, Hosea, Joel, Amos, Obadiah, Jonah, Micah, Nahum, Habakkuk, Zephaniah, Haggai, Zechariah, Malachi, **New Testament:** Matthew, **Mark**, Luke, John, Acts, Romans, 1&2 Corinthians, Galatians, Ephesians, Philippians, Colossians, 1&2 Thessalonians, 1&2 Timothy, Titus, Philemon, Hebrews, James, 1&2 Peter, 1,2&3 John, Jude, Revelation.

More Data Books, chapters and verses actually make it easier to find things in the Bible. When this investigation is finished you will remember that the stories discovered are in the Book of Mark. Mark is the second book of the New Testament. The Bible is God's word to us. The gospels are full of true life stories of people that Jesus met. We will investigate some of them in this book... it's amazing to realise that these things really happened and that every word from God is true!

 That's great Click. Thanks for showing us that. So come on everyone - pick up a pencil, think sharp and let's go.

JOHN THE BAPTIST

God spoke about John through a man called Isaiah, hundreds of years before John was born. Let's use Click to show us what was said.

I will send my messenger ahead of you, who will prepare your way - a voice of one calling in the desert, Prepare the way for the Lord. Make straight paths for him."

And it's true. John did live in the desert. He wore clothes made of camel's hair and a leather belt, and he ate locusts and wild honey. He preached that people should turn away from their sins so that they could be forgiven.

Lots of people came to hear John. They came from Jerusalem and the Judean countryside. Many said that they were sorry for their sins and were baptised in the River Jordan. But John's purpose was to talk about someone else much more important - a man named Jesus.

"After me will come one more powerful than I, whose sandals I am not worthy to stoop down and untie. I baptise you with water, but he will baptise you with the Holy Spirit."

So, John was a ... well, let's find out. Answer the questions, and the vertical column will reveal what you need to know.

1. John's clothes were made from the skin of this animal. Mark 1:6
2. People travelled from here to hear John. Mark 1:5
3. He said that John was to come. Mark 1:2
4. John lived here. Mark 1:4
5. Jesus would do this with the Holy Spirit. Mark 1:8
6. Food John ate. Mark 1:6
7. In Mark 2:7 what can God alone do for sin?
8. Name one person who was baptised by John in Mark Chapter 1:9
9. A river where people were baptised. Mark 1:9

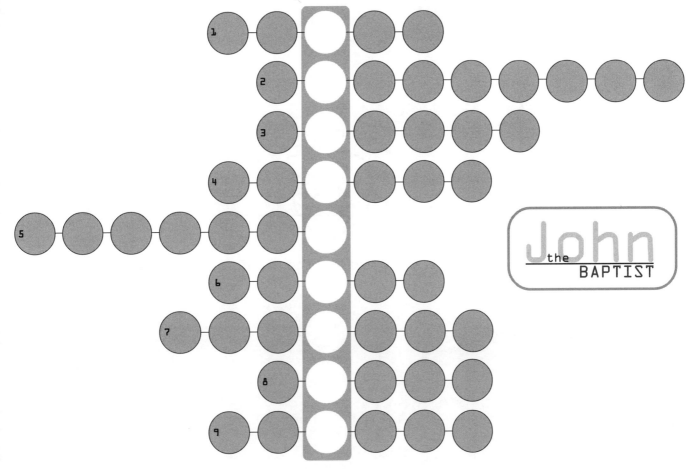

John
the
BAPTIST

And one of the things you're going to notice as we investigate this book is how fast everything will go. Mark's gospel is action packed and fast paced - it was almost as if he was in a rush when he was writing. So come on everyone - pick up the pace and let's go!

BAPTISM OF JESUS

We've found more information about John. And we reckon that the most awesome day of his life was when Jesus came and asked John to baptise him.

That's right Harry. It's amazing, because as Jesus was coming out of the water it seemed as if heaven was torn open, and the Holy Spirit came upon him like a dove.

And then a voice could be heard from heaven. Want to know what it said? Well, use the code and find out. After that, Jesus disappeared into the desert and lived among the wild animals.

Yeah. Forty days he was there for. And God sent angels to look after him. But come on, let's hurry and find out what Jesus did afterwards...

KEY

A B C D

E F G H

I J K L

M N O P

Q R S T

U V W X

Y Z

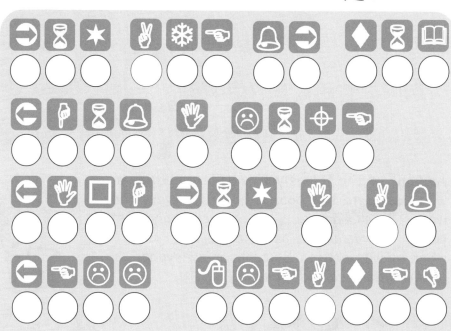

6

HEALING OF LEPER

We've been finding out lots from Mark's gospel. Like, what people thought of Jesus when he started his ministry. It seems like they couldn't get enough of him. He was like a magnet.

He did such amazing things – preached, healed the sick, performed miracles. You could tell that he really cared about people. And of course, good news travels fast. Well, see for yourself. Here's one story from our files.

DETAILS: Testimony of leper healed by Jesus
PROOF: local priest who examined him after the healing.

Last week I was desperate. You see, I had a terrible disease called leprosy, and it was eating away at my body bit by bit. I looked awful! No-one would come near me in case they caught it – and who could blame them – I used to think the **same.** **Anyway, I couldn't** work and I had to <u>rely</u> on others to leave me food. **It** was really scary. One of the things we all dread had happened to me, and now I **felt** desperately alone.

...Until I met Jesus! As soon as I saw him **I** knew that he cared – you **could** see it in his eyes. It was as if he knew me – knew all my worries and fears and understood. I fell down on my knees in desperation and begged him to heal me. Then he touched me!! "Be clean," he said, and that was all it took. Suddenly, my skin was smooth – I was healed. Jesus told me not to tell anyone, but how could I keep quiet? I was so **excited,** no-one could **silence** me. My life has changed and I have God to thank for it.

Take the first letter of each highlighted word and find out what the man offered to God after he was healed.

Answer: _ _ _ _ _ _ _ _ _ _ _

JESUS HEALS A PARALYTIC

The investigation is going on at a cracking pace. Here we are in Chapter 2 already! So Harry - what has Click sniffed out for us this time?

Well, Jess, it looks really interesting... we've got some pictures here for the Detectives to look at. See if you can find the mouse who is hiding in each of the pictures!

"Here we are inside a house in Capernaum. It's packed out with people. Can you guess why?"

"That's right! Jesus is in there. But, hang on a minute. Who's that on the roof?

"Amazing! They've lowered a paralysed man on a stretcher through the roof. Reports are coming through that Jesus has healed him."

"Look! The people are praising God. Jesus told the paralysed man that his sins were forgiven and to take up his mat and go home. And here he is."

Good work Click! Oh... and Click says to tell the other detectives there's a puzzle to be found on the next page! Here are two clues to get you started... Jesus has the authority to forgive our sins... and in Mark Chapter two Jesus said two things to the paralysed man. Once you've done the puzzle - look up the chapter to check your work.

A	B	C	D	E	F	G	H	I	J	K	L	M

N	O	P	Q	R	S	T	U	V	W	X	Y	Z

Jesus'
Heals

1

2

9

HEALING ON THE SABBATH

Here's a story about a man whom Jesus healed on the Sabbath. Unjumble the words and put them in the right places. You can find the story in Mark Chapter 3.

Synagogue live
shrivelled angry
trouble stubborn
lawful Stretch
Sabbath Pharisees

Jesus went into the

_ _ _ _ _ _ _ _ _ and met a man

with a _ _ _ _ _ _ _ _ _ hand.

There were some people there who

didn't like Jesus. They wanted to

cause _ _ _ _ _ _ _ so they watched

to see if Jesus would heal the man.

If he did, they could accuse him

of breaking one of their rules.

Jesus told the man to stand up.

Then he said, "Which is _ _ _ _ _ _

on the _ _ _ _ _ _ _ : to do good or

to do _ _ _ _ _ , to save life or kill?"

But they didn't say anything.

Jesus looked around and was

_ _ _ _ _. He was very upset

because they were so

_ _ _ _ _ _ _ _. He said to the

man "_ _ _ _ _ _ _ out your hand."

The man stretched it out and it

was healed. Then the

_ _ _ _ _ _ _ _ _ _ went out and

began to plot how they might kill

Jesus.

APPOINTING OF APOSTLES

Hey Harry - look at this! Jesus chose twelve men to be his particular friends and helpers. They were called disciples or apostles.

Yes - and it was Jesus who trained them and then sent them out to preach. He even gave them authority to drive out demons! Now Click has printed off a word search for us to do. Can you find the names of the disciples hidden below?

Matthew, Bartholomew, Peter,
Thaddeus, Judas Iscariot,
John, Thomas, Philip
Andrew, James
James, Simon (the Zealot)

Mark 3

SELECTING THE **APOSTLES**

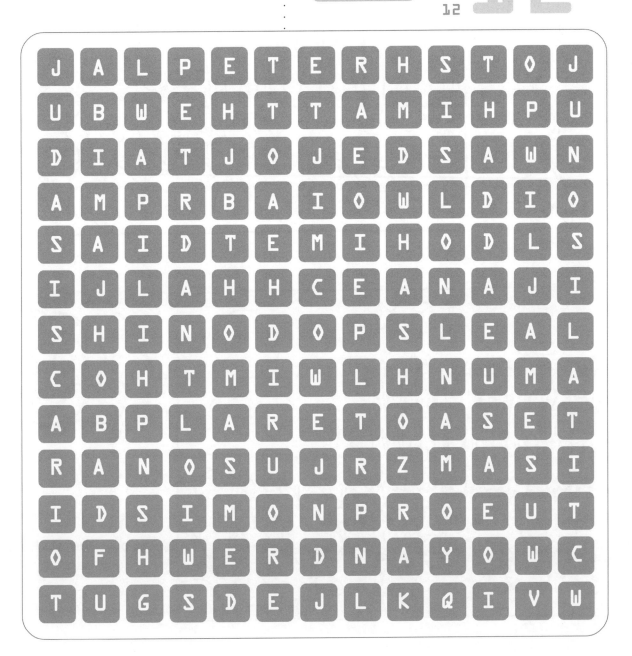

J	A	L	P	E	T	E	R	H	S	T	O	J
U	B	W	E	H	T	T	A	M	I	H	P	U
D	I	A	T	J	O	J	E	D	S	A	W	N
A	M	P	R	B	A	I	O	W	L	D	I	O
S	A	I	D	T	E	M	I	H	O	D	L	S
I	J	L	A	H	H	C	E	A	N	A	J	I
S	H	I	N	O	D	O	P	S	L	E	A	L
C	O	H	T	M	I	W	L	H	N	U	M	A
A	B	P	L	A	R	E	T	O	A	S	E	T
R	A	N	O	S	U	J	R	Z	M	A	S	I
I	D	S	I	M	O	N	P	R	O	E	U	T
O	F	H	W	E	R	D	N	A	Y	O	W	C
T	U	G	S	D	E	J	L	K	Q	I	V	W

PARABLE OF THE SOWER

Wherever Jesus went, lots of people came to hear him speak. And one day, it got so crowded that he had to get into a boat on a lake.

Jesus told people stories to help them understand more about God, and one of them was about a sower. Before you read the story - check out these pictures. There are several differnces for you to spot....

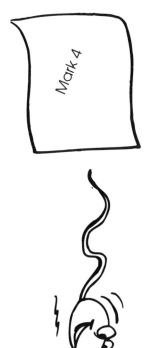

Mark 4

Go to the next page to read the story!

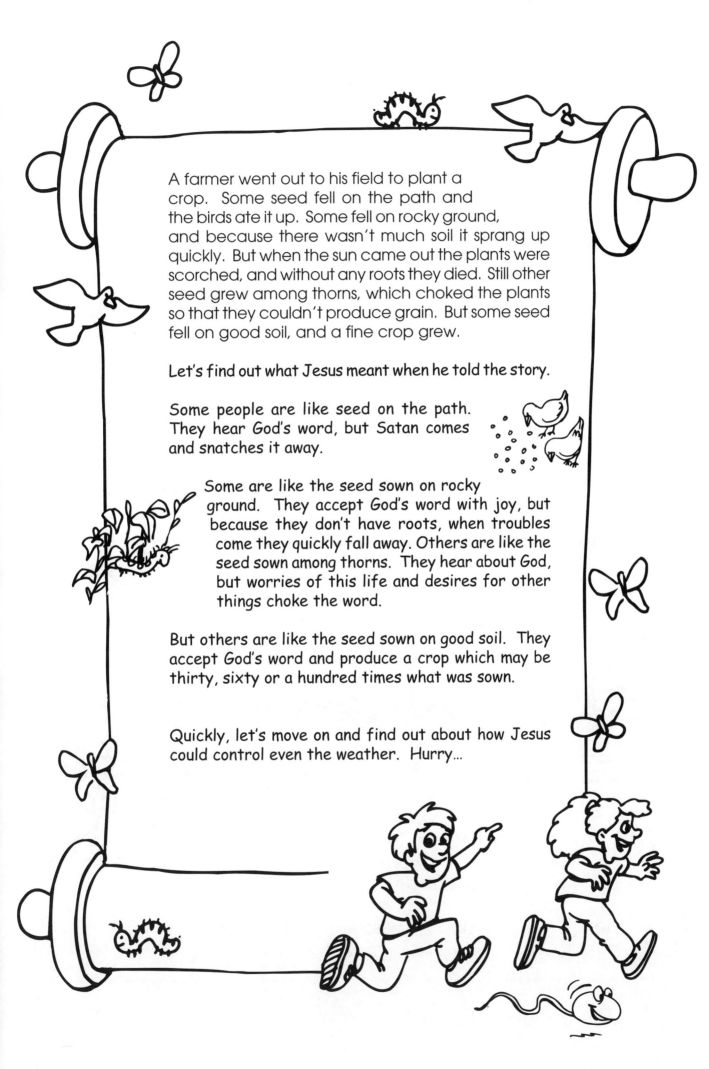

A farmer went out to his field to plant a crop. Some seed fell on the path and the birds ate it up. Some fell on rocky ground, and because there wasn't much soil it sprang up quickly. But when the sun came out the plants were scorched, and without any roots they died. Still other seed grew among thorns, which choked the plants so that they couldn't produce grain. But some seed fell on good soil, and a fine crop grew.

Let's find out what Jesus meant when he told the story.

Some people are like seed on the path. They hear God's word, but Satan comes and snatches it away.

Some are like the seed sown on rocky ground. They accept God's word with joy, but because they don't have roots, when troubles come they quickly fall away. Others are like the seed sown among thorns. They hear about God, but worries of this life and desires for other things choke the word.

But others are like the seed sown on good soil. They accept God's word and produce a crop which may be thirty, sixty or a hundred times what was sown.

Quickly, let's move on and find out about how Jesus could control even the weather. Hurry...

JESUS CALMS THE STORM

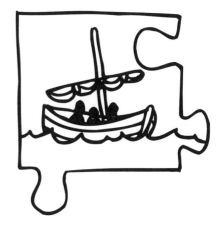

Oops. These jigsaw pieces have become muddled. Can you match the right sentence with each picture?

1. Jesus was crossing a lake with his disciples.

2. There was a terrible storm that evening.

3. The waves broke over the boat and nearly swamped it.

4. The disciples were afraid and woke Jesus, who was sleeping.

5. Jesus said, "Quiet! Be still!" and the storm ended.

6. Jesus said, "Why are you frightened? Have you still no faith?"

Now that you've matched all the pictures and the words turn the page to page 16 and fill in the story from memory.

The disciples were terrified. Unscramble the words to find out what they said.

nEve   het   niwd   nad   vesaw   yboe   mhi.

_____   ___   ____   ___   _____

____   ___

14

DEMON-POSSESSED MAN'S HEALING

Phew! Those disciples really thought they'd had it, didn't they Jess?

They still had so much to learn. And so do we Harry! It's Mark Chapter 5 already! Come on detectives let's find out what else they did while they were in Galilee.

It all began after Jesus and his disciples had crossed Lake Galilee to the region of the Gerasenes. There was a man living there among the tombs and in the hills and he had an evil spirit. His name was Legion and he was very strong. I mean, take a look at this...

Pretty scary!

Anyway, this man Legion ran out to meet Jesus, when he got to him, he fell on his knees. "What do you want with me, Jesus, Son of the Most High God," he shouted. Those demons didn't stand a chance. Jesus commanded them to come out of Legion, and they went into a herd of pigs. The pigs rushed into the Lake and were drowned.

And Legion? Well he was completely changed. Jesus does that to people. Legion was free of the evil spirits. Jesus broke the power of sin. He can break the power of sin in our lives too. But you'd think that the townspeople would have been pleased to see Legion back to normal, but instead they were really scared. In fact, they begged Jesus to leave. But Legion was different to the others. God had changed his life and he begged Jesus to let him go with him. Solve the puzzle on page 17 to see what Jesus said to him.

Memory Challenge
(from page 14)

Jesus was c _ _ _ _ _ _ _ _ a _ _ _ _ with his

d _ _ _ _ _ _ _ _ _. There was a terrible S_ _ _ _

that _ _ _ _ _ _ _ _. The _ _ _ _ _ _ broke over the

_ _ _ _ and nearly _ _ _ _ _ _ _ _ it.

The d _ _ _ _ _ _ _ _ _ were _ _ _ _ _ _ _ and

woke _ _ _ _ _ _ , who was _ _ _ _ _ _ _ _ _ _.

_ _ _ _ _ _ said, "_ _ _ _ _ _! Be _ _ _ _ _!"

and the _ _ _ _ _ _ ended. Jesus said, "Why are
you

_ _ _ _ _ _ _ _ _ _ _?

Have you still _ _ _ _ _ _ _ _?"

What did Jesus say?

6am 2pm   7am 2pm 12pm 4am

7pm 2pm   11pm 2pm 8pm 5pm

5am 12am 12pm 8am 11am 11pm   12am 1pm 3am

7pm 4am 11am 11am   7pm 7am 4am 12pm   7am 2pm 10pm

12pm 8pm 2am 7am   7pm 7am 4am   11am 2pm 5pm 3am

7am 12am 6pm   3am 2pm 1pm 4am   5am 2pm 5pm

11pm 2pm 8pm   12am 1pm 3am   7am 2pm 10pm

7am 4am   7am 12am 6pm   7am 12am 3am

12pm 4am 5pm 2am 11pm   2pm 1pm   11pm 2pm 8pm

SENDING OUT OF DISCIPLES

Let's move on. We're onto Mark Chapter 6 now. You see, it was time for Jesus to send out his disciples. They had to put into practice what he'd taught them. Here are two disciples. Help them to find their way to the next town.

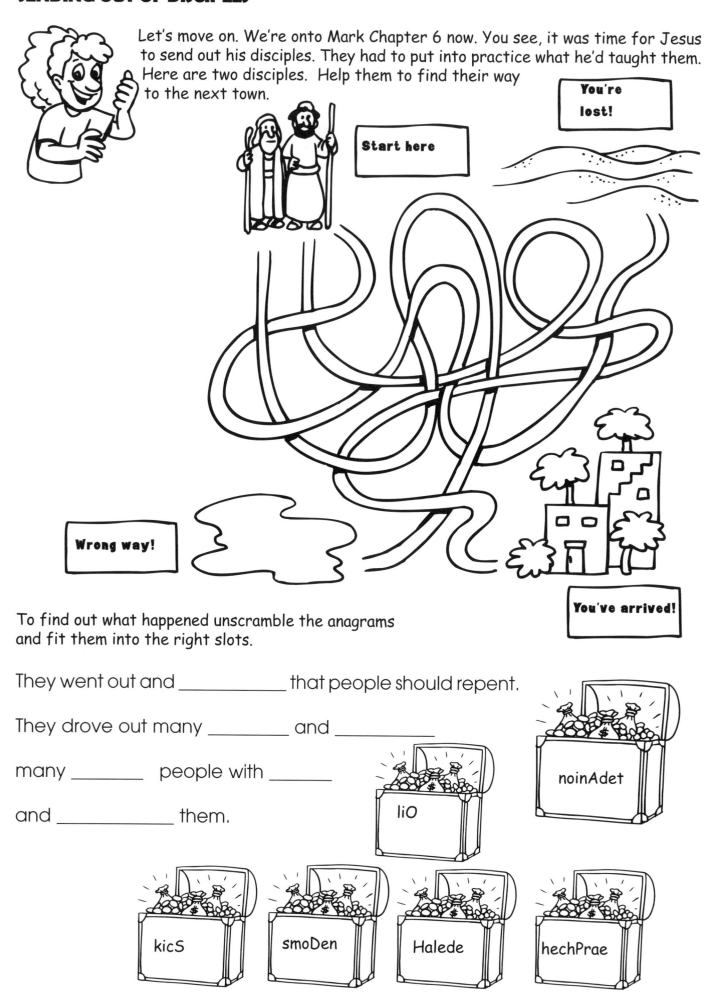

You're lost!

Start here

Wrong way!

You've arrived!

To find out what happened unscramble the anagrams and fit them into the right slots.

They went out and _____ that people should repent.

They drove out many _____ and _____

many _____ people with _____

and _____ them.

liO

noinAdet

kicS

smoDen

Halede

hechPrae

FEEDING THE FIVE THOUSAND

Look at this Harry things are going at as fast a pace as usual. Now the disciples all came back to report to Jesus about what they'd been teaching and doing. It was a busy and exciting time - and because many people were coming and going they didn't even have time to eat.

Mark 6

HOLY BIBLE

Jesus knew that they all needed to get some rest, so they took a boat and headed for a solitary place. But the people who saw them leaving guessed where they were going and ran on foot from the towns. Soon a large crowd was waiting for Jesus. You'd think that Jesus would have been dismayed when he saw the crowds. But instead, he felt compassion for the people because they were like sheep without a shepherd. It wasn't long before he began to teach them.

Well, by this time it was getting late in the day and the disciples came to Jesus. "It's already very late," they said. "Why not send the people to the villages and countryside around us so that they can buy something to eat." You can imagine how puzzled they must have felt when Jesus replied, "You give them something to eat."

"But it would take eight months of a man's wages to feed these people. Are we to go and buy that much and give it to them?" they asked.

Jesus asked how many loaves they had, and when they had found out, they said, "Five - and two fish." Then Jesus told them to sit everyone down in groups, and looking up to heaven, he gave thanks and broke the bread. He also divided the two fish among them all. It was a miracle. Everyone ate and was satisfied, and after they had eaten, the disciples picked up twelve basketfuls of broken pieces of bread and fish. The number of people who had eaten the meal was five thousand.

How well do you know this story? See if you can complete the crossword. It's on the next page...

Across

1. No time to do this. Mark 6:31
2. How many loaves? Mark 6:38
5. There were two. Mark 6:38
7. How many baskets of food were left? Mark 6:43
10. Broken pieces of this were left over. Mark 6:43
11. Jesus looked up to it. Mark 6:41
12. A lonely place (8) Mark 6:32
14. Jesus cared for the people like one. Mark 6:34

Down

1. How many month's wages? Mark 6:37
2. The people arrived on——(4) Mark 6:33
3. Places to buy food. Mark 6:36
4. The people were like these animals. Mark 6:34
6. They waited for Jesus. Mark 6:34

8. There were five. Mark 6:38
9. Jesus gave it before breaking the bread. Mark 6:41
10. A means of transport. Mark 6:45
13. The people did this to get to Jesus. Mark 6:33

Did you get that? Terrific! Well, there's still so much more to tell you. Let's crack on and I'll tell you about the time Jesus gave the disciples a fright.

FEEDING THE 5000

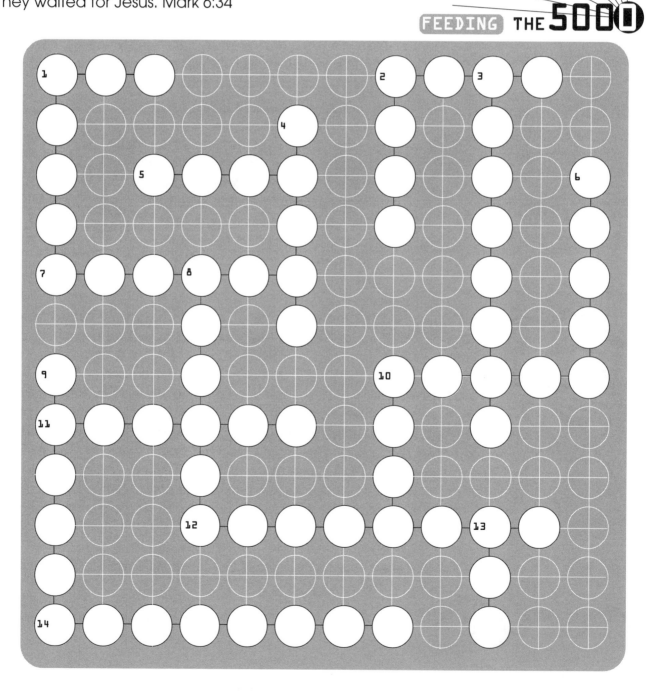

JESUS WALKS ON WATER

This is the last story in Mark Chapter 6. Phew - this is hard work. Being a detective isn't an easy job. Have you ever been out in a boat on a windy day? It's hard work if you're trying to row - which is just what the disciples were trying to do one evening. There they were, straining away at the oars, when suddenly they had a real fright. From out of nowhere a ghostly figure appeared and started walking towards them on the water. Pretty terrifying! And not surprisingly they shouted with fright. What was it? Who was it? It was scary.

Have you guessed yet? It was Jesus! He spoke to them straight away, saying, "Take courage. It is I. Don't be afraid." And the next thing they knew, he was climbing into the boat with them and the wind was dying down.

So that was it. They just continued across the lake and then dropped anchor.

So now it's Quick Question Time. Turn the page and see how fast can you answer the next set of questions? When you've finished, read the vertical column and find out the name of the place where they landed.

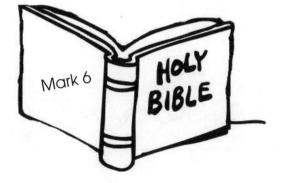

Mark 6

HOLY BIBLE

Quick Questions

1. What did the disciples think they were seeing? Mark 6:49

2. Who was the mistaken identity? Mark 6:45-51

3. They did this to stop the boat from drifting. Mark 6:53

4. What was against the rowers? Mark 66:48

walking on WATER

5. The time of day. Mark 6:47

6. Who was in the boat when it set out? Mark 6:45

7. The disciples felt this when they saw the figure. Mark 6:50

8. They were told to take ———. Mark 6:50

9. The disciples continued across it. Mark 6:47

10. Jesus could walk on it. (Look at title)

SYRO-PHOENICIAN WOMAN

Mark 7

Wow we're onto Mark Chapter 7 now. We've got to hurry on. So much to do ... On to a house at Tyre. Follow Click and off we go!

Here we are. Jesus didn't want anyone to know that he was in the house. But, you've guessed it. Someone found out! What happened next? Follow Click onto the next bit of the story... he's in a bit of a rush so watch out!

And this person looks as if she is in a bit of a rush too. Something must be worrying her.... I wonder what it is?

She was a Greek woman, and she begged Jesus to cast a demon out of her daughter. Now turn the page to find out what happened next.

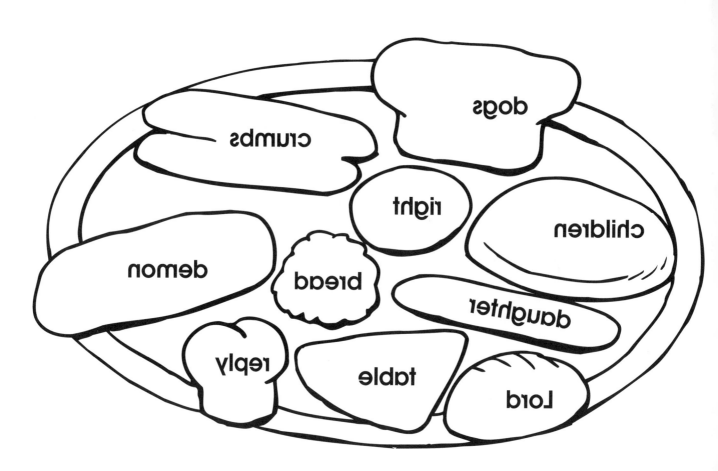

Jesus tested the woman. The words in the picture above are all back to front. Can you work out what each word would be if it was the right way round? Then fill in the spaces to see what he said.

Jesus said, "First let the _ _ _ _ _ _ _ _ eat all they want, for it is not _ _ _ _ _ to take the children's _ _ _ _ _ and toss it to their _ _ _ _ ."
"Yes, _ _ _ _ ," she replied, "But even the dogs under the _ _ _ _ _ eat the children's _ _ _ _ _ _ ."

Then he told her, " For such a _ _ _ _ _ you may go; The _ _ _ _ _ has left your _ _ _ _ _ _ _ _ ."

And the lady went home and found her child lying on the bed, and the demon had gone.

HEALING OF THE DEAF AND MUTE MAN

Chapter 7 is coming to an end now... with a miracle. Can you imagine what hope Jesus brought to sick people. He could change lives, as the deaf and mute man in this story was to discover.

Jesus left Tyre and went to Decapolis where a man was brought to him. The man was deaf and could hardly talk, and the people begged Jesus to place his hand on him.

Jesus took the man away from the crowd and put his fingers into the man's ears. He spat and touched the man's tongue, then he looked up to heaven and said with a deep sigh, "Be opened." Straight away, the man's ears were opened and he began to speak.

Jesus commanded the people not to tell anyone, but they couldn't help talking about it.

And now for another puzzle... On the next page answer the questions. Use the number code to find out what the people said about Jesus.

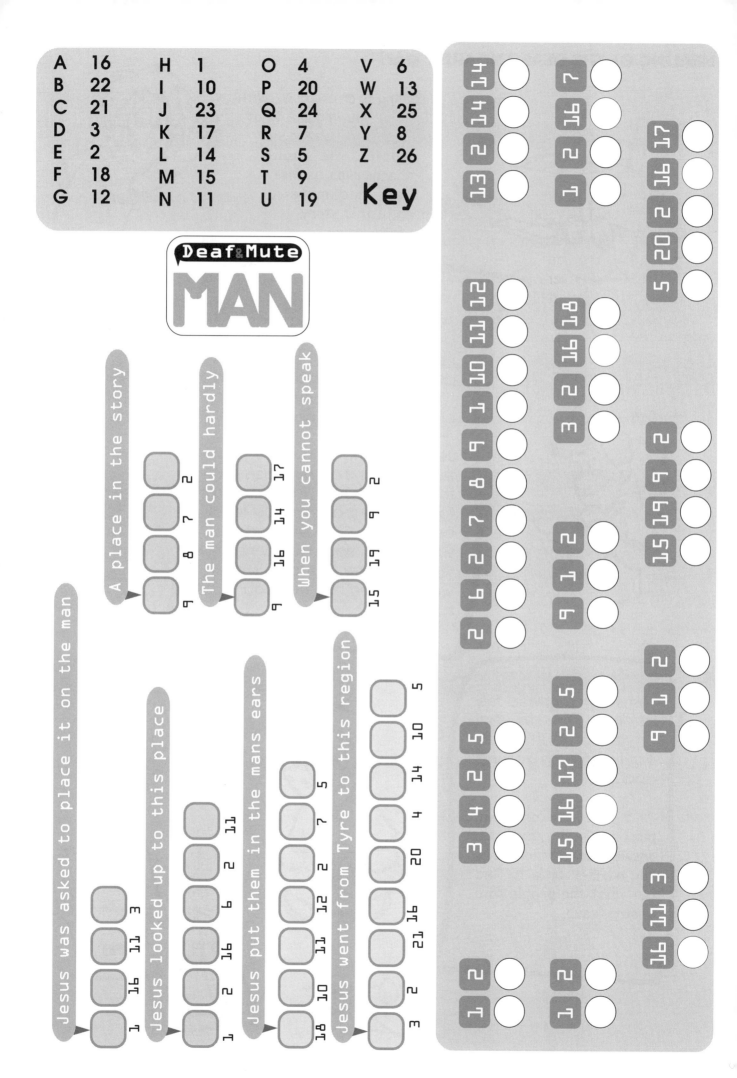

FEEDING A VERY LARGE CROWD

Jesus is good at meeting people's needs. In Mark chapter 8 we find him feeding yet more people! One thing you find in the gospels is that the same stories are told by different people. This story appears in Matthew and Mark. Another large crowd had gathered to hear Jesus speak and he was concerned that they didn't have any food. Jesus asked the disciples how many loaves they had - they replied, "Seven." Jesus took the loaves and gave thanks and broke them along with a few small fish. How would that feed so many people? Well it did. The disciples handed out the food and there was enough for everyone. Even after everyone had eaten the left overs filled seven baskets. After that Jesus got into a boat with his disciples and went to the region of Dalmanutha.

Answer the questions, and the vertical columns will reveal the number of people, besides women and children, who ate.

1. The disciples had a few. Mark 8:7
2. The place where the crowds came to Jesus. Matthew 15:29
3. The people felt this. Mark 8:3
4. The people did this to God when they saw what Jesus did. Matthew 15:31

1. How many days had they been with Jesus? Mark 8:2
2. Jesus gave it before they ate. Mark 8:6
3. Jesus was concerned that the people would do this if they didn't have food. Mark 8:3
4. They were healed. Mark 7:37
5. How many baskets left? Mark 8:8
6. The people felt this way. Matthew 15:31
7. They were healed. Matthew 15:30
8. They gave out the food. Mark 8:6

Look out for the other Bible Detectives book on Matthew and read about how Matthew tells the same story.

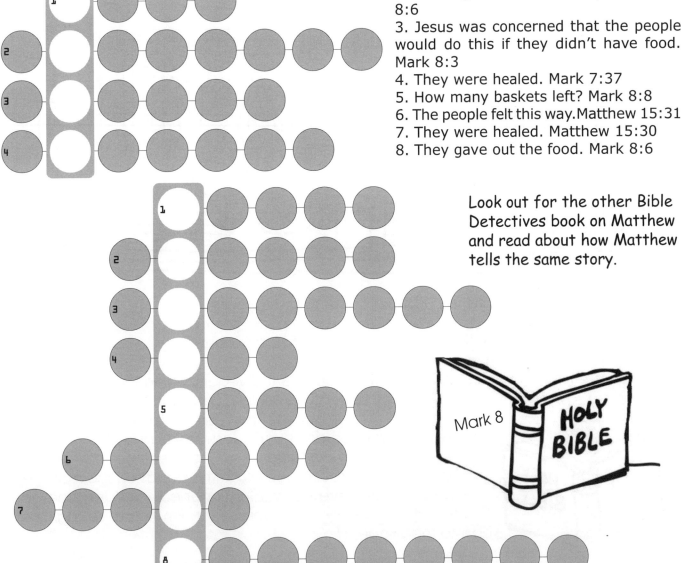

HEALING OF BLIND MAN

Here we are at Bethsaida where a crowd of people are waiting for Jesus and the disciples. Can you lead the blind man through the village to the crowds.

Well done. Mission accomplished! Now let's hear what happened.

Well, the blind man obviously had some good friends, because when Jesus arrived, they were determined that Jesus should heal him. They must have wondered then, why Jesus took their friend outside the village. When they had got away from the hustle and bustle of the village, Jesus turned to the man and spat on his eyes. Then he put his hands on him. "Do you see anything?" Jesus asked. And the man looked up and said, "Yes. I can see people - they look like trees walking around." Jesus put his hands on the man's eyes again, and they were completely opened. Suddenly he could see everything clearly. Then Jesus sent him home, saying, "Don't go into the village."

Mark 8   HOLY BIBLE

PETER'S CONFESSION OF CHRIST

It was time to move on to some villages around Caesarea Philippi. While they were on their way, Jesus asked a big question. "Who do people say I am?" Crack the code and find their answers hidden in the text below.

uqog   uca   lqjp   vjg   dcrvkuv

....

....

uqog   uca   gnklcj

....

....

uqog   uca   qpg   qh   vjg   rtqrjgvu

....

....

Jesus said, "But what about you? Who do you say I am?"
Use the same code to find Peter's answer hidden below:

Aqw ctg vjg ejpkuv

a	y
b	z
c	a
d	b
e	c
f	d
h	f
i	g
j	h
k	i
l	j
m	k
n	l
o	m
p	n
q	o
r	p
s	q
t	r
u	s
v	t
w	u
x	v
y	w
z	x

And Jesus warned them not to tell anyone about him.

29

THE TRANSFIGURATION

Jesus took Peter, James and John with him up a high mountain. And as they stood together Jesus was transfigured before them and his clothes became dazzling white. Then Elijah and Moses appeared and they talked to Jesus. Pretty frightening for the disciples, but Peter was quick to say something. "Rabbi, it's good for us to be here. Let me make three shelters one for you, one for Moses and one for Elijah." Peter didn't really know what to say because they were all so frightened.

Then a cloud appeared and surrounded them, and a voice came out of it, saying, "This is my son whom I love. Listen to him." Suddenly, when Peter, James and John looked round they saw no-one but Jesus.

When they returned back down the mountain, Jesus gave them orders to tell no-one what they had seen until.... to find out when the disciples were allowed to tell people what they had seen solve the following puzzle...

Jesus gave them orders not to tell anyone what they had seen ...

Mark 9:9

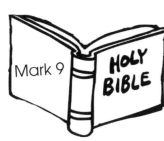

Mark 9 / HOLY BIBLE

CROSSWORD

Across

1. It enveloped them. Mark 9:7
4. Listen to - - - (3) Mark 9:7
6. What came out of the cloud? Mark 9:7
8. Mark and Matthew both did this.
W _ _ _ _ a gospel.
9. Where did Jesus take Peter James
and John? Mark 9:2
12. A disciple Mark 9:2
13. A name for Jesus. Mark 9:5
14. He disappeared. Mark 9: 4&8
16. They weren't built. Mark 9:5

Down

5 &2. This is my - - - whom I - - - - Mark 9:7
3. A command made by the voice. Mark 9:7
7. They were dazzling. Mark 9:3
10. How many shelters? Mark 9:5
11. A disciple. Mark 9:2
12. God's son. Mark 9:7-8.

THE
transfiguration

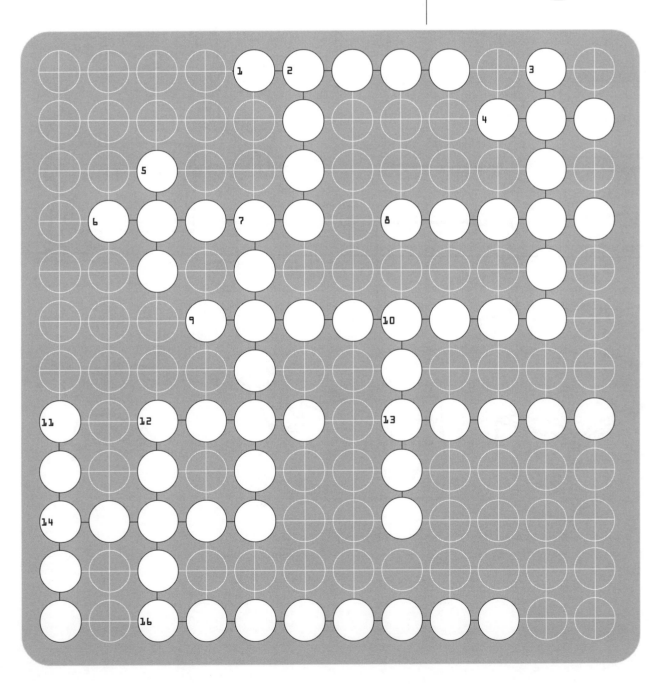

LITTLE CHILDREN TO JESUS

It's another chapter change and we're onto Chapter 10. Things are going fast here. Hey Harry - Click says there's some other children today to help us with the investigation. They're part of the puzzle...

Yes, Jess, that's right, they're here because people liked to bring their children to Jesus. Mark Chapter 10 has an amazing story in it about Jesus and some little children. Jesus loved children and would take them in his arms, put his hands on them and bless them. But the disciples weren't so friendly. Once, when people brought their children to Jesus the disciples told them off. Jesus was very indignant about it. To find out what he said, rearrange the signs into the right order. Click has a clue... he says to watch the actions of the children... they will give you a hint as to what words come after each other

and do not

Let the little

of God

for the kingdom

come to me,

hinder them

children

belongs to

Mark 10   HOLY BIBLE

such as these

_ _ _   _ _ _   _ _ _ _ _ _   _ _ _ _ _ _ _ _

_ _   _ _ _   _ _ _ _ _ _   _ _ _ _ _   _ _

_ _ _ _ _ _   _ _   _ _ _   _ _ _ _ _ _ _

_ _ _ _ _   _ _   _ _ _ _ _   **Mark 10: 14**

32

And Jesus went on to say.... to find out what he says do the puzzle again... remembering the actions of the characters are giving you a clue to the order of the words...

receive the

like a

I tell you the truth

Kingdom

will not

of God

will never enter it

Anyone who

little child

_ ____ ___ ___ ____

_____ ___ ____ ___ _____

___ _____ __ ___ ____ _

_____ ____ ____ _____

_____ __ __ Mark 10:15

Did you get that? Well done... so now we've got to pick up the pace again. Click says we've another two stories to cover in Mark chapter 10. We'd better step on it!

33

THE RICH YOUNG MAN

Are you still with us? Great. Come on then and read a story about a man who loved his money.

A rich young man ran up to Jesus one day and fell on to his knees. "Good Teacher. What must I do to inherit eternal life?" he asked.

Jesus replied, "Why do you call me good? No-one is good except God. You know the commandments," he said, "Do not murder, do not commit adultery, do not steal, do not testify falsely, do not cheat. **Honour** your father and mother."

"Teacher," said the man, "I have kept all these commandments since I was a boy."

Jesus looked at the man and loved him. "There is one thing missing," he said "Go and sell **everything** you have **and** give it to the poor. Then you will have treasure in heaven. Then come, follow me."

The man's face fell for he was **very** rich, and he went away sad. Jesus said to his disciples. "How hard it is for the rich to **enter** God's kingdom. It is easier for a camel to go through the eye of a **needle** than for a rich man to enter the kingdom of God."

The disciples were amazed. "Then who could possibly be saved?" they asked.

Jesus looked at them and said, "Humanly speaking it's impossible, but not with God; all things are possible with God." Jesus also said, "Everyone who has left home or brothers or sisters or mother or father or children or fields for me and the Good News will receive a hundred times more, and they will have eternal life. But many who seem to be first now will be the last, and those who are thought to be the least important here will be the greatest then.

Great story Jess... so let's go through it again and take the first letter from every highlighted word and write them in the spaces in the verse below. This verse is from Matthew and it teaches us that earthly treasures like money and possessions do not last. Instead we should love and obey God so that we have will have a treasure that lasts for ever... the missing word in the verse tells us where this treasure will be.

Do not store up for yourselves treasures on earth where moth and rust destroy and thieves break in and steal. But store up for yourselves treasures in __ __ __ __ __ __ where moth and rust do not destroy and where thieves do not break in and steal. For where your treasure is there your heart will be also. Matthew 6:19-21

Look at this Harry! Click's downloaded another puzzle for us. Come on Bible Detecives let's see if we can answer the following questions. The vertical column will reveal a special gift which God will give to those who love him.

1. A name given to Jesus. Mark 10:17
2. God told us not to do it. Mark 10:19
3. It would be a big squeeze to get it through this eye. Mark 10:25
4. We are forbidden to do this. Mark 10:19
5. Something we should do to our parents. Mark 10:19
6. We may have this in heaven. Matthew 6:20
7. The rich man was told to do this with his possessions. Mark 10:21
8. You might leave these for the sake of Jesus and the Good News. Mark 10:29
9. Not poor. Mark 10:25
10. They will be last. Mark 10:31
11. A sharp tool mentioned in the story. Mark 10:25

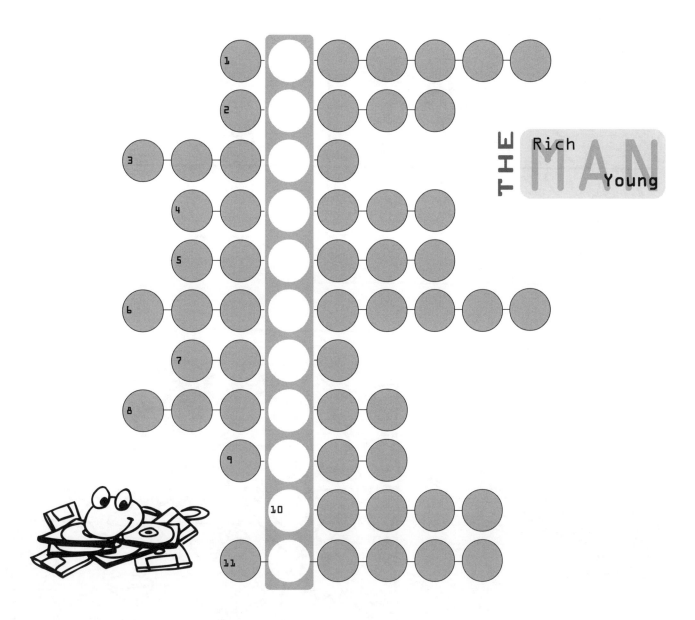

THE **MAN** Rich Young

BLIND BARTIMAEUS

Come on Jess - Click says we've got to get on the move. Jesus was always on the move. And it was while he was leaving the city of Jericho that he met Bartimaeus. Let's press on and find out what happened. Jess knows all about it.

That's right Harry! Well, you can imagine what it must have been like. Another hot, dusty day with the usual crowd pressing in on Jesus and the disciples. It must have been noisy, but it didn't stop Jesus from hearing Bartimaeus. "Jesus, son of David," he cried out. "Have mercy on me."
Now Bartimaeus was blind, and he had been begging by the roadside. He was just a nobody to some in the crowd, and they tried to shut him up. "Shh, don't bother him," they said, but he had caught Jesus' attention.
It must have felt great when Jesus called Bartimaeus over. He didn't waste time. Throwing aside his cloak, he jumped to his feet and pushed his way through to Jesus. "I want to see," he cried when Jesus asked what he wanted.
"Go," said Jesus. "Your faith has healed you." And straight away, Bartimaeus received his sight and followed Jesus along the road.

Bartimaeus must have jumped for joy when he found he could see again. Here are two pictures of Bartimaeus doing just that. See if you can spot the four differences between them.

THE TRIUMPHAL ENTRY

Hey Harry, that's Click on the phone and he says that this is us on to Mark Chapter 11 already! Jesus and his disciples have arrived at the Mount of Olives outside Jerusalem. Jesus then sent two of his disciples to the village ahead and told them that they would find a colt there which no-one had ever ridden. They were to untie it and bring it to him.

Right then... Click has just emailed us with the instructions for the next puzzle. We're to take a look at the picture and see if we can find five flowers.

Jesus told the disciples, "If anyone asks what you are doing, say, "The Master has need of it and will send it back shortly."

The disciples did as Jesus asked, and when the people asked what they were doing with the colt, they answered as Jesus had told them. When they got back, the disciples threw cloaks over the colt and Jesus sat on it. Lots of people threw their coats on the road, and others spread branches out from the field. The people who went ahead and who followed Jesus called out, "Hosanna" and "Blessed is he who comes in the name of the Lord," and "Hosanna in the highest."

TAXES TO CAESAR

Now we've made a quick move onto Mark chapter 12. We're meeting up with some of the people who didn't like Jesus. One day some religious people called Pharisees and some supporters of the leader Herod came. They tried to butter up Jesus and trap him into saying something which could get him arrested. Tell us Jess, what was it that the Pharisees asked Jesus?

Well, the question they asked was, "Is it right for us to pay taxes to the Roman government or not?" Jesus knew that they were trying to trick him and told them so. "Show me a Roman coin and I'll tell you," he said. "Whose picture and title are stamped on it?" "Caesar's," they replied.

Jesus gave a very clever answer to their question. Can you unscramble the anagrams that are around the edges of the coins to find out what he said.

Mark 12:17

THE GREATEST COMMANDMENT

We're still on Mark Chapter 12. But do you know the greatest commandment Jesus gave? He was in the temple when a teacher of the law asked him, "Of all the commandments which is the most important?"

"The most important one," Jesus replied, "is this: 'Hear O Israel, the Lord our God, the Lord is one. Love the Lord your God with all your...." to finish off what Jesus said copy all the letters except X Y and Z from the picture and place them in the spaces marked out below.

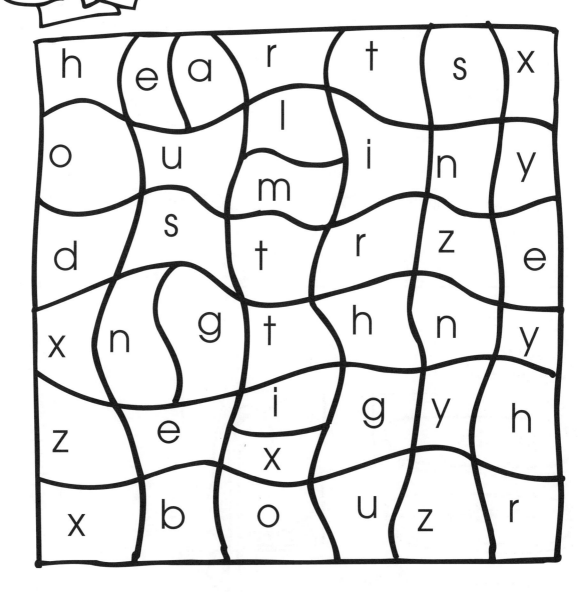

Love the Lord you God with all your _ _ _ _ _ and with all your _ _ _ _

and with all your _ _ _ _ and with all your _ _ _ _ _ _ _ _. The second is

this: Love your _ _ _ _ _ _ _ _ _ as yourself. There is no commandment

greater than these. Mark 12: 29-31

THE WIDOW'S OFFERING

Click has just downloaded this picture for us. It is a picture of what the collection box in the temple might have looked like. Lots of people came here to drop in their money. Some did this to show other people how wealthy they were. Others because they wanted people to think they were very good. Other people just did it just because they wanted to please God and to obey him. And it was while Jesus was here one day that a poor widow came and put in two copper coins. They were worth only part of a penny. Not a lot, you might think, but Jesus knew otherwise.

Slot the words on the steps below into the right spaces and find out what Jesus said. Then colour in the picture.

This _ _ _ _ _ _ _ _ _ _ has put _ _ _ _ into the

treasury than all the _ _ _ _ _ _ _. They all gave out of

their _ _ _ _ _ _ _ but she, out of

her _ _ _ _ _ _ _ _, put in

_ _ _ _ _ _ _ _ _ _ _ _ ~ all

she had to _ _ _ _ on.

Poor

poverty

everything

others

more

live

wealth

Widow

Mark 12

JESUS ANOINTED AT BETHANY

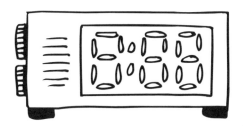

Right then, Click is telling us that we really have to speed up. So Bible Detectives let's put time on fast forward and go to chapter 14. So let's turn back the clock and find out what happened two days before the Jewish Passover Celebration and Feast of Unleavened Bread.

Well, Harry, it appears that there is still a bit of a problem with the Pharisees. The religious leaders and teachers of religious law were still looking for a chance to secretly capture Jesus and put him to death. However, they decided not to do it during the Passover or there might be a riot.

Jesus was in **Bethany** at the home of Simon, a man who had leprosy. While he was there, a woman came with an alabaster jar of very **expensive** perfume. She broke the jar and poured the perfume on Jesus's head.

Some of the people there were very unhappy about this. "Why was this perfume wasted?" **they** asked. "She could have sold it for more than a year's wages and given the money to the poor." They scolded the woman harshly.

Well, Jesus wasn't at all impressed with them. "Leave her alone," he **replied**. "She has done a beautiful thing to me. You will always have the poor among you and you can help them at any time. But you will not always have me." Jesus went on, "She has **anointed** my body for burial ahead of time, and "I tell **you** the truth, "Wherever the gospel is preached throughout the world this woman's deed will be told of in her memory."

After this, Judas Iscariot, one of the disciples, went to the leading priests... to find out what it is that Judas Iscariot actually does once he gets there - take the first letter from each of the highlighted words and insert them into the gaps below.

Judas Iscariot went to the leading priests

to ▢ ▢ ▢ ▢ ▢ Jesus.

Answer the questions, then find your answers hidden in the wordsearch

1. The jar was made of this. Mark 14:3

2. The perfume was not cheap. Mark 14:3

3. A disease mentioned in the story. Mark 14:3

4. The woman did this to the jar. Mark 14:3

5. A feast beginning with the letter P. Mark 14:1

6. They are always with us. Mark 14:7

7. How many days before the feast? Mark 14:1

8. It was poured onto Jesus's head. Mark 14:3

anointing

9. The woman had done this for burial ahead of time.
Reverse the following letters (detnionA)

10. The leaders were afraid of one. Mark 14:2

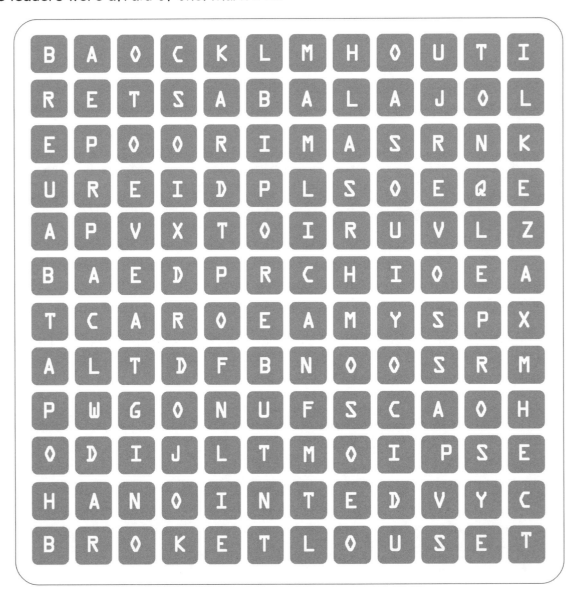

B	A	O	C	K	L	M	H	O	U	T	I
R	E	T	S	A	B	A	L	A	J	O	L
E	P	O	O	R	I	M	A	S	R	N	K
U	R	E	I	D	P	L	S	O	E	Q	E
A	P	V	X	T	O	I	R	U	V	L	Z
B	A	E	D	P	R	C	H	I	O	E	A
T	C	A	R	O	E	A	M	Y	S	P	X
A	L	T	D	F	B	N	O	O	S	R	M
P	U	G	O	N	U	F	S	C	A	O	H
O	D	I	J	L	T	M	O	I	P	S	E
H	A	N	O	I	N	T	E	D	V	Y	C
B	R	O	K	E	T	L	O	U	S	E	T

JESUS PREDICTS PETER'S DENIAL

Jesus told his disciples that they would all fall away from him. Then he told them that after he had risen, he would go ahead of them to Galilee. Peter was positive that he wouldn't deny Jesus. "Even if everyone falls away I will not," he declared. But Jesus replied, "I tell you the truth. Tonight, before the cockerel crows twice, you will disown me three times."

Peter insisted, "Even if I have to die with you, I will never disown you." Peter did deny Jesus and what Jesus said came true. Before the cockerel crowed twice Peter had denied Jesus three times. After all his bold boasts he couldn't even tell other people that he knew Jesus Christ. He lied and said that he had never even met him. Below is a silhouette picture of a cockerel in the early morning. See if you can match up the shapes in the picture with the pictures placed below. Only one picture from each set is correct. The story continues on the following page where you can follow the story of the Garden of Gethsemane by going around the garden yourself.

Watch out for the eight shy birds and the sleeping disciples.

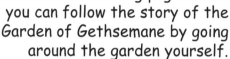

THE LORD'S SUPPER

So what story has Click got for us today Jess?

Well Harry - It was the first day of the Feast of Unleavened Bread, and at this time it was usual to sacrifice a Passover lamb. The disciples were wondering what to do, so they said to Jesus, "Where shall we go to make preparations for the Passover?" Jesus said to two of his disciples, "Go to the city where you will meet a man carrying a jar of water. Follow him and say to the owner of the house he enters, "The teacher asks, 'where may I eat the Passover with my disciples?' You will be shown a large upper room which will be furnished and ready. Make preparation for us there."
The disciples did as Jesus said and prepared the Passover.
Help the man with the jar to guide the disciples to the right house.

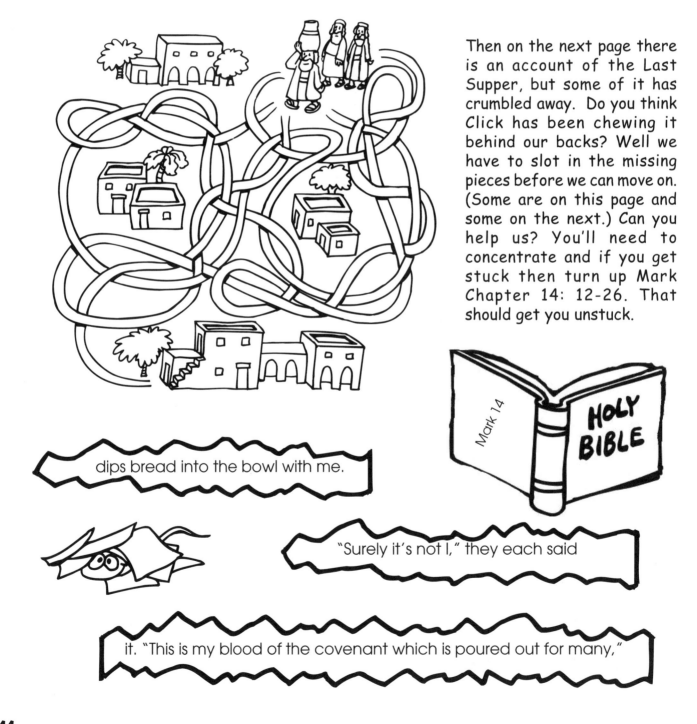

Then on the next page there is an account of the Last Supper, but some of it has crumbled away. Do you think Click has been chewing it behind our backs? Well we have to slot in the missing pieces before we can move on. (Some are on this page and some on the next.) Can you help us? You'll need to concentrate and if you get stuck then turn up Mark Chapter 14: 12-26. That should get you unstuck.

Mark 14

HOLY BIBLE

dips bread into the bowl with me.

"Surely it's not I," they each said

it. "This is my blood of the covenant which is poured out for many,"

Evening came and Jesus arrived at the upper room with his disciples. While they were eating Jesus said, "I tell you the truth, one of

The disciples were saddened

one by one. "It is one of the twelve" he said, "and one who

Woe to that man. It would be better if he had never been born. As they ate Jesus took

it, this is my body. Then Jesus took a cup, gave thanks, and offered it to them and they all drank from

he said. "I will not drink it again until the day when I drink it in the kingdom of God." They sang a hymn and went out to the Mount of Olives.

you will betray me, one who is eating with me.

bread, gave thanks and broke it "Take

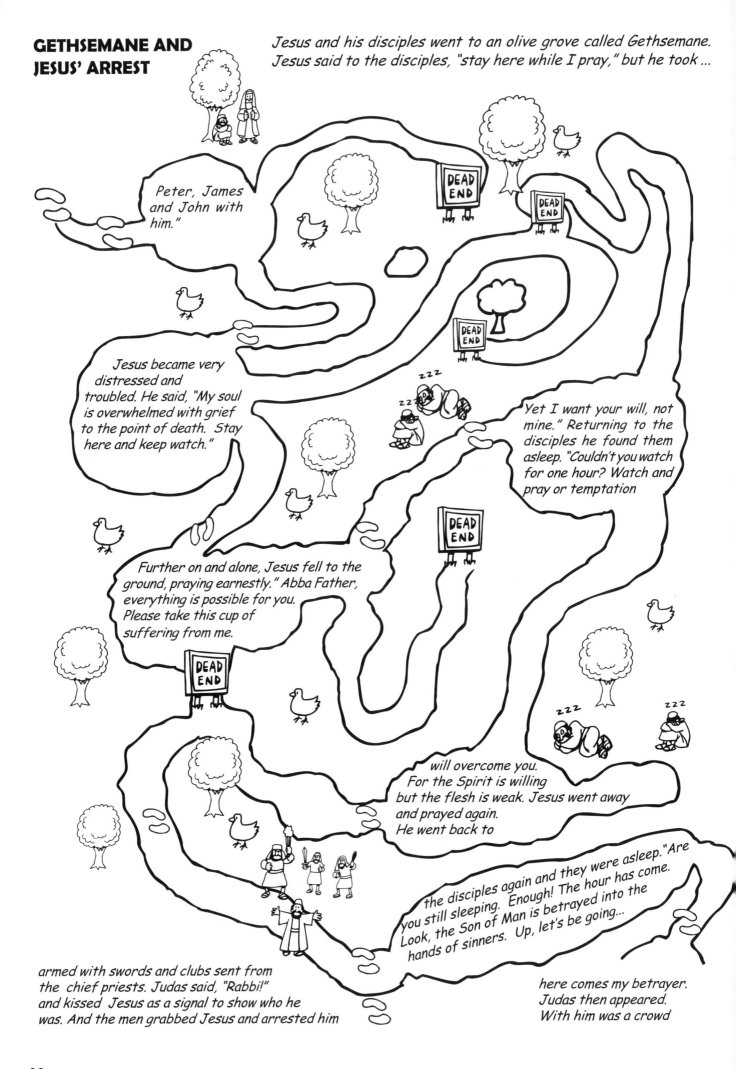

GETHSEMANE AND JESUS' ARREST

Jesus and his disciples went to an olive grove called Gethsemane. Jesus said to the disciples, "stay here while I pray," but he took ...

Peter, James and John with him."

Jesus became very distressed and troubled. He said, "My soul is overwhelmed with grief to the point of death. Stay here and keep watch."

Yet I want your will, not mine." Returning to the disciples he found them asleep. "Couldn't you watch for one hour? Watch and pray or temptation

Further on and alone, Jesus fell to the ground, praying earnestly." Abba Father, everything is possible for you. Please take this cup of suffering from me.

will overcome you. For the Spirit is willing but the flesh is weak. Jesus went away and prayed again. He went back to

the disciples again and they were asleep. "Are you still sleeping. Enough! The hour has come. Look, the Son of Man is betrayed into the hands of sinners. Up, let's be going...

DEAD END

armed with swords and clubs sent from the chief priests. Judas said, "Rabbi!" and kissed Jesus as a signal to show who he was. And the men grabbed Jesus and arrested him

here comes my betrayer. Judas then appeared. With him was a crowd

JESUS BEFORE THE COUNCIL

Look Click's got a code for us to crack. It's about Jesus when he was taken to the High Priest's house. The leading priests and teachers of religious law had been trying to find people to tell lies about Jesus so that they could put him to death. The High Priest asked Jesus what he had to say for himself, but he would not reply. Jesus was asked, "Are you the Messiah, the Son of God?" Use the code to find out what Jesus replied. The High Priest showed his horror at Jesus' reply by tearing his clothing. "Why do we need witnesses," he said. "This is blasphemy." And they all condemned Jesus to death.

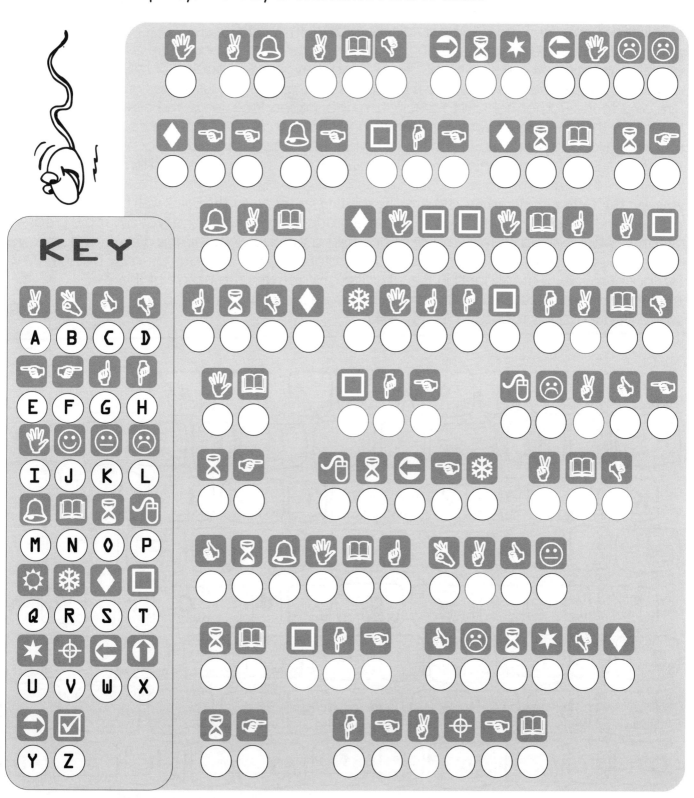

TRIAL BEFORE PILATE

Things were happening very quickly now.

Very early the next day, Jesus was taken to Pilate, the Roman governor. "Are you the King of the Jews?" Pilate asked Jesus. "Yes, it is as you say," he replied. The leading priests then accused Jesus of many crimes, but Jesus would say nothing.

The Passover was a special feast that the Jews celebrated and each year, it was the governor's custom at Passover time to release a prisoner. But when he asked the crowd, they had been stirred up by the leading priests to demand the release of Barabbas. Pilate asked, "What shall I do with this man you call King of the Jews?" and they shouted back, "Crucify him!" Pilate was anxious to please the crowd so he set Barabbas free, ordered Jesus to be flogged, and turned him over to the Roman soldiers to crucify him. The soldiers took Jesus and called out the whole battalion. They dressed him in a purple robe and made a crown of long, sharp thorns. Then they shouted, "Hail, King of the Jews" and spat on him and beat him on the head with a stick. When they had finished mocking him, they put his own clothes on again and led him away to die.

Answer the following questions and slot the missing letters into the brick wall below. All answers can be found in Mark Chapter 15. Who were the group of mockers?; Who was a people pleaser?; What was happening at the time of year when a prisoner was released?; What name was given to Jesus?; What is the name of a royal colour?; Jesus was punished by being?; What symbol of royalty is mentioned in the chapter?; What was the name of the ex-convict?; They were sharp and painful. What were they?; The governor was urged to do this to Jesus. What was it?

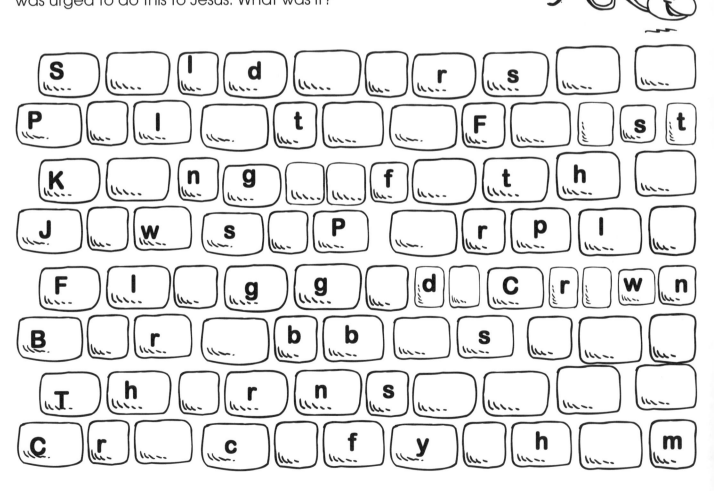

48

JESUS'S CRUCIFIXION

In Jesus's time, death by hanging on a cross was the worst form of punishment for a criminal. It was also one of the most painful ways to die. This is what happened ...

A man called Simon who was from Cyrene in north Africa had come into Jerusalem, and he was forced to carry Jesus's cross. Jesus was taken to a place called Golgotha, which means Skull Hill (or place of the skull). He was offered a drink of wine and myrrh, but he would not take it. Then he was nailed to the cross. Meanwhile, the soldiers gambled to decide who would get Jesus's clothes.

The crucifixion took place at 9 o'clock in the morning. A sign was placed over Jesus's head. It read, "The King of the Jews."

On either side of Jesus were two criminals who were crucified with him.

Jesus was mocked by the passers-by and the leading priests and teachers of the law. They shouted, "He saved others but he can't save himself." They even told him to prove that he was the King of Israel by coming down from the cross.

KING OF THE JEWS

Mark 15

Now take the first letter of the first answer, the second of the second answer and so on to find a name to describe Jesus. Click has already filled in one or two of the letters to give you a head start!

1. The soldiers and priests did this to Jesus. Mark 15:20 & 31
2. The city in which Jesus was when he was arrested. Mark 15:41
3. God's Son. Mark 15:37-39
4. Jesus was invited to come down from it. Mark 15:32
5. What happened to Jesus and the two criminals. Mark 15:32
6. Simon was from this continent.
(See above story.)
7. Skull Hill. Matthew 15:22

Jesus'
CRUCIFIXION

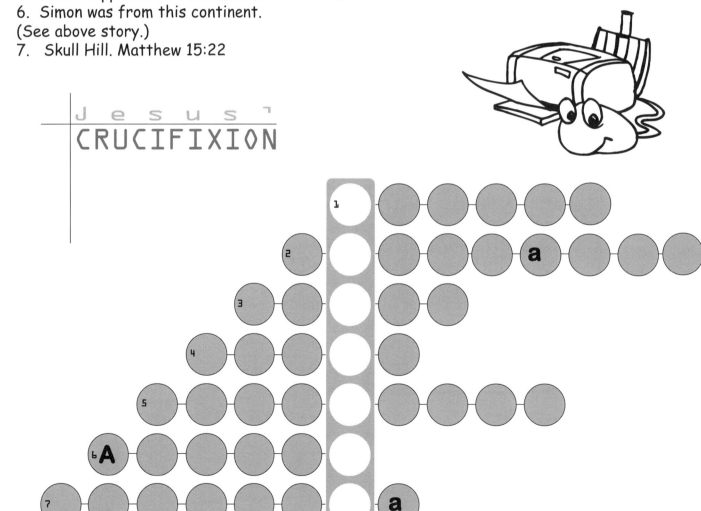

JESUS' DEATH

What do you think about this part of the story Jess? It's not the happy ending that I thought it was going to be?

Don't worry Harry... other people thought the same as you when Jesus died... but Jesus death isn't the end of the story... We just have to read on. It's not long now until the end of chapter 15 and then it's one more chapter before the end of the book of Mark. Let's see what Click has downloaded for us from the Bible today... Here's the Bible story and look - there's another code to crack so let's get to work.

At noon darkness fell and it lasted until 3 o'clock. Then Jesus cried out, "My God, My God, Why have you forsaken me?"

Some of the onlookers misunderstood Jesus and thought that he was calling for the prophet Elijah. Then one of them filled a sponge with sour wine and held it up to him on a stick so that he could drink. Jesus uttered a loud cry and then he died. The curtain in the temple was torn in two from top to bottom.

A Roman officer had faced Jesus and seen how he died, and he declared...

Click says if you want to find out what the Roman officer said use the key to crack the code.

KEY

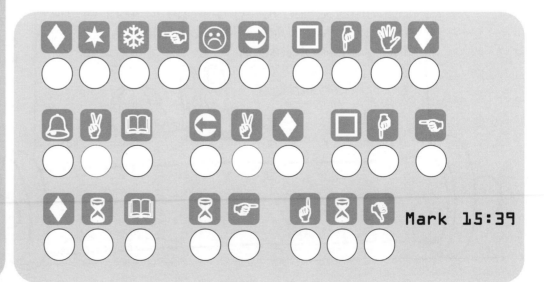

Mark 15:39

JESUS' BURIAL

Come on Detectives ... let's pick up the pace for the last couple of pages. Alot has happened and just like Harry - you might be thinking that everything has gone wrong... but keep going there's a big surprise about to arrive. Read the story and then work out the maze quiz on the other page

Jesus death happened on a Friday, the day before the Sabbath. This day had a special name for the Jewish people it was called the preparation day. Then as evening approached a man named Joseph of Arimathea, who was an important member of the Council summoned up the courage to go to Pilate and ask for Jesus' body.

When Joseph told Pilate that Jesus was dead and that he wanted to take his body away for burial Pilate was very surprised. He hadn't expected Jesus to be dead already. Pilate then called for the officer in charge, who confirmed it.

Joseph was given permission to take Jesus' body. So he brought a sheet of linen cloth, and taking Jesus' body down from the cross, he wrapped him in it. Then he laid the body in a tomb carved out of rock and rolled a stone in front of the entrance. Mary Magdalene and Mary the mother of Joseph saw where Jesus' body had been laid.

Now decide whether the sayings on the next page are true or false. If the answer is Yes then follow the route that says Yes. If it goes to a dead end then you've made the wrong decision. If it carries onto the next statement then you've done well and you should keep going!

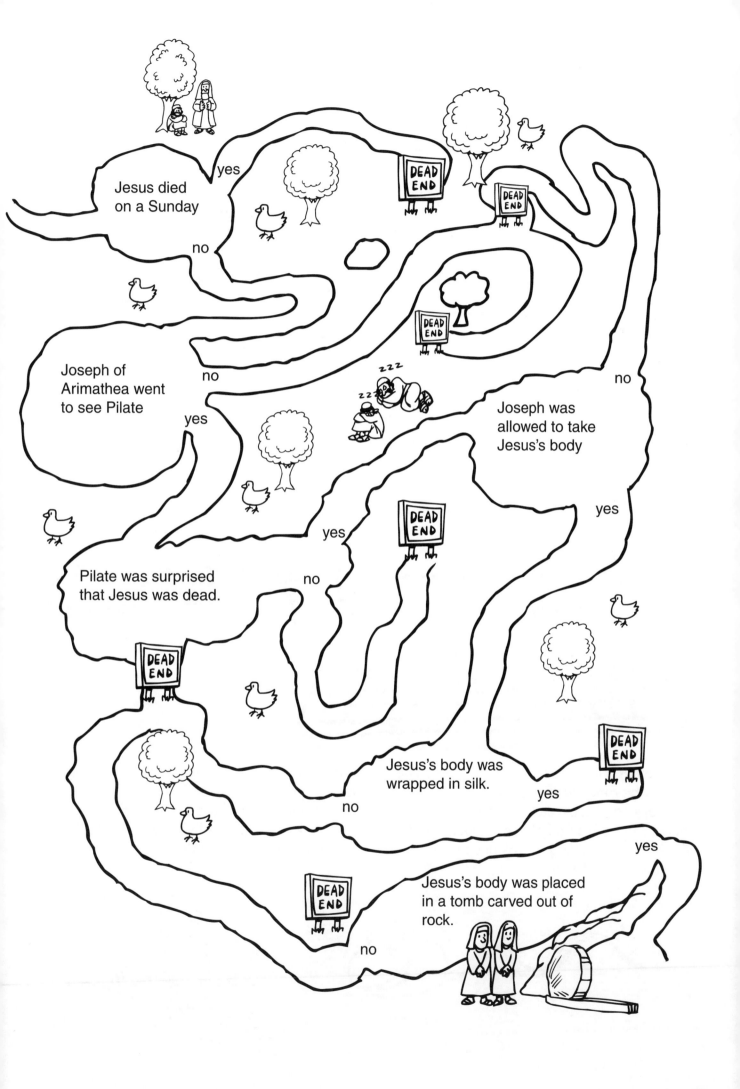

Jesus died on a Sunday

yes

no

Joseph of Arimathea went to see Pilate

no

yes

Joseph was allowed to take Jesus's body

no

yes

Pilate was surprised that Jesus was dead.

yes

no

Jesus's body was wrapped in silk.

no

yes

Jesus's body was placed in a tomb carved out of rock.

no

yes

DEAD END

And look at this Jess now we've come to the last page! And it's the best bit! The next evening after the Sabbath had ended, Mary Magdalene and Salome and Mary the mother of James went out to buy burial spices to put on Jesus's body.

So you can imagine their surprise when the following sunrise they found that the stone had been rolled away from the tomb. This is what happened.

The women entered the tomb where they found an angel clothed in white. "Do not be surprised," he said. "You are looking for Jesus of Nazareth who was crucified. He isn't here. He has been raised from the dead. See, this is where they laid his body. Then the angel said, "Go and give this message to the disciples, including Peter. Jesus is going ahead of you to Galilee and you will see him there.

Log on next time!
See you soon,
Click :-)

The women fled trembling from the tomb and they gave Peter and the disciples the message. Later, they met with Jesus, and he sent them out to preach the Good News of Salvation and eternal life. Jesus was taken up to heaven and sat down in the place of honour at God's right hand.... and after all these happenings took place Mark was guided by God to write it down... which is how we've got this gospel which we've just investigated! That's all for now folks - see you again next time!

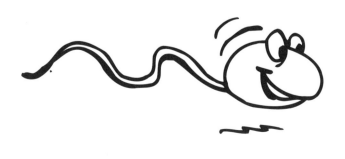

Certificate of Recognition

As an official member of the
Bible Detectives Squad
you have been awarded this certificate
to mark an excellent result!

Name _____

Investigation _____

Commenced on: _____

Completed on: _____

Signature: _____

Answers: Page numbers in bold. 5: 1.Camel 2. Jerusalem. 3. Isaiah. 4.Desert. 5. Baptise. 6. Honey. 7. Forgive. 8. Jesus. 9. Jordan. **6**: You are my son whom I love, with you I am well pleased. **7**: sacrifices **9**: Son your sins are forgiven; Get up, take your mat and go home." **10**: Jesus went into the Synagogue and met a man with a shrivelled hand. There were some people there who didn't like Jesus. They wanted to cause trouble so they watched to see if Jesus would heal the man. If he did, they could accuse him of breaking one of their rules. Jesus told the man to stand up. Then he said, "Which is lawful on the sabbath : to do good or to do evil , to save life or kill?" But they didn't say anything. Jesus looked around and was angry. He was very upset because they were so stubborn. He said to the man "Stretch out your hand." The man stretched it out and it was healed. Then the Pharisees went out and began to plot how they might kill Jesus. **11**: Wordsearch**12**: Spot the differences - Bird has changed position; Butterflies in one picture not in other; Worm has changed position; Mouse has changed position; Caterpillar is different shape in one picture to the other and is in different place. **14** Even the wind and the waves obey him. **17**: Go home to your family and tell them how much the Lord has done for you and how he has had mercy on you. **18**: Preached; demons; anointed; sick; healed; oil. **20**:Across 1.eat 2. five 5. Fish 7. twelve 10. bread 11. heaven 12. Solitary 14. Shepherd Down 1. Eight 2. Foot 3. Villages 4.Sheep 6. Crowd. 8. Loaves 9. Thanks 10. Boat 13. Ran. **22**: 1. ghost 2. Jesus 3.anchored 4. wind 5. Evening 6. disciples 7. afraid 8. Courage 9. Lake 10. Water/Gennesaret **24**: Jesus said, "First let the children eat all they want, for it is not lawful to take the children's bread and toss it to their dogs." "Yes, Lord," she replied, "But even the dogs under the table eat the children's crumbs." Then he told her, " For such a reply you may go; The demon has left your daughter." **26**: Hand; Heaven; Fingers; Decapolis; Tyre; Talk; Mute; He does everything well. He makes the deaf hear and the mute speak. **27**: 1. Fish 2. Mountain 3. Hungry 4. Praised 1. Three 2.Thanks 3. Collapse 4. Mute 5. Seven 6. Amazed 7.blind 8. Disciples/Four Thousand. **29**: Some say John the Baptist; some say Elijah; some say one of the prophets; You are the Christ.

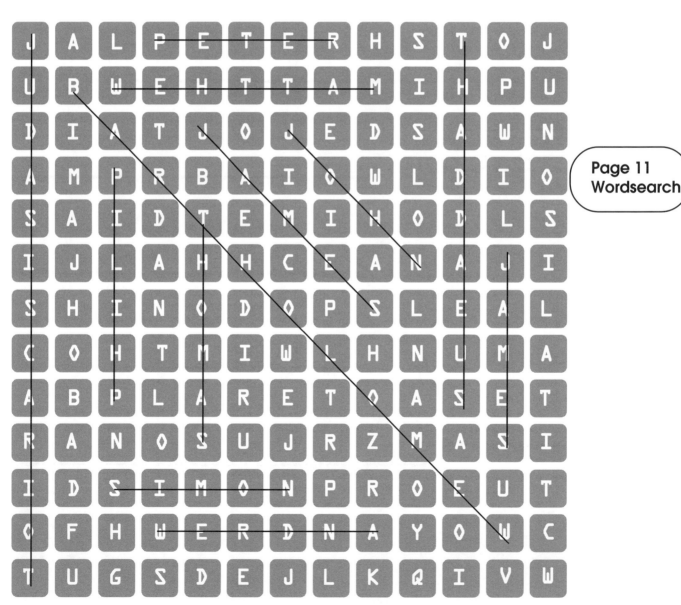

Page 11
Wordsearch

30: Jesus gave them orders not to tell anyone what they had seen until the Son of Man had risen from the dead. **31:** Across 1. cloud 4. him 6. voice 8. Wrote. 9. mountain 12. John 13. Rabbi 14. Moses 16. Shelters Down 5&2. Son; Love 3. Listen 7. Clothes 10. Three 11. James 12. Jesus **32:** Let the little children come to me, and do not hinder them, for the kingdom of God belongs to such as these. **33**: I tell you the truth, anyone who will not receive the kingdom of God like a little child will never enter it. **34** heaven. **35:** 1. Teacher 2. Steal 3. Camel 4. Murder 5. Honour 6. Treasure 7. Sell 8. Fields 9. Rich 10. First 11. needle - Eternal life. **36:** Spot the differnces - flower, hat, begging bowl, man's expression. **38:** "Give to Caesar what is Caesar's and to God what is God's." **37:** Flowers are found as follows- one on window; one in donkey's mouth; one on man's belt; one on side of house and one at the foot of the pictures. **39**: heart; soul; mind; strength; neighbour. **40:** This poor widow has put more into the treasury than all the others. They all gave out of their wealth but she, out of her poverty, put in everything - all she had to live on. **41:** betray **42:** 1. alabaster 2. Expensive 3. Leprosy 4. Broke 5. Passover 6. Poor 7. Two 8. Perfume 9. Anointed 10. Riot **44&45:** Evening came and Jesus arrived at the upper room with his disciples. While they were eating Jesus said, "I tell you the truth, one of you will betray me, one who is eating with me. The disciples were saddened. Surely it's not I, they each said one by one. "It is one of the twelve," he said, "and one who dips bread into the bowl with me. Woe to that man it would be better if he had never been born." As they ate Jesus took bread, gave thanks and broke it. "Take it, this is my body." Then jesus took a cup, gave thanks, and offered it to them and they all drank from it. "This is my blood of the covenant which is poured out for many," he said. "I will not drink it again until the day when I drink it in the kingdom of God." They sang a hymn and went out to the Mount of Olives. **47:** Iam and you will see the Son of Man sitting at the right hand of the Mighty One and coming on the clouds of heaven." **48:** Soldiers; Pilate; Feast; King of the Jews; Purple; Flogged; Crown; Barabbus; Thorns; Crucify him. **50:** 1. Mocked 2. Jerusalem 3.Jesus 4.Cross 5.Crucified 6. Africa 7. Golgotha/Messiah **51**: Surely this man was the Son of God

Page 42 Wordsearch

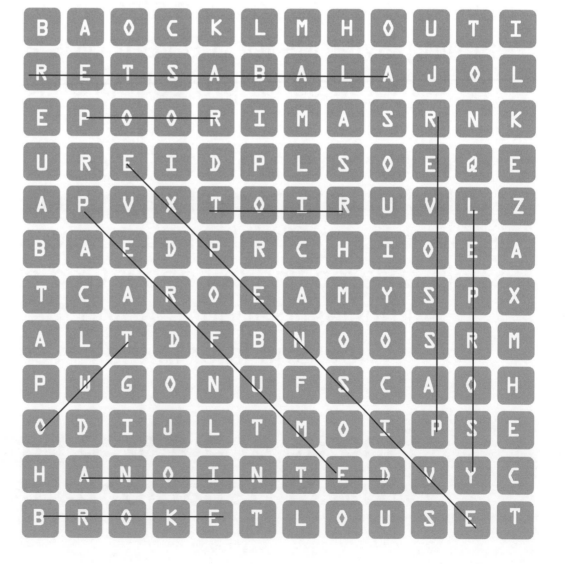